LIVING LONG AGO
TRAVEL AND TRANSPORT

Helen Edom

Edited by Cheryl Evans

Designed by Brian Robertson

Illustrated by Chris Lyon, Teri Gower and Guy Smith

Consultant: Dr Michael Hitchcock

Series consultant: Dr Anne Millard

KT-415-985

Contents

Language adviser: Betty Root M.B.E.

Early travellers

Long ago, people got food by hunting wild animals and picking nuts and berries. They walked from place to place to find their food.

They carried everything they owned with them, and camped in caves or shelters.

People had to watch out for dangerous animals.

Basket of spare clothes

They put things into baskets and bags to make them easier to carry.

People could drag baskets and bags on a frame made of branches.

Using animals

Later, people became farmers. They kept animals and grew plants for food. They used animals to help carry their harvest and other things.

They put loads on a wooden sledge. They tied the sledge to their animals and got them to pull it along.

Some farmers fixed round wooden shapes under the sledge to help it go more easily. These were the first wheels.

Their tools were made of stone. They were heavy.

Two could carry a heavy bag between them on a pole.

Making baskets and bags

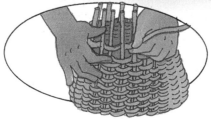

People made baskets by weaving bendy twigs together. Baskets are still made like this today.

They made bags by sewing animal skins together. They used long needles shaped out of bone.

Travelling over water

All over the world people made boats so they could cross water or travel swiftly down rivers and streams.

The simplest boats were ▶ logs tied together to make a raft. These were paddled along with branches.

◀ Dug-outs were made by hollowing out logs. People lit a fire to burn out the centre. Afterwards, they scraped out the burnt bits.

Some people tied bundles ▶ of reeds together to make a boat. Here you can see one kind used in South America.

◀ Others stretched skins over a round wooden frame. This made a boat called a coracle. They smeared tar over it to keep water out.

Near the North Pole, people ▶ used a narrow skin boat called a kayak. This was fast and easy to steer. Eskimos still use them nowadays.

Make a model coracle

You need a plastic bag, pipe cleaners, scissors, stiff card and sticky tape.

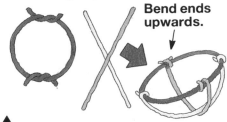

Bend ends upwards.

▲
Twist two pipe cleaners together to make a circle. Make two others into a cross. Fix the cross on to the circle as shown.

Frame

Cut a sheet of plastic from the bag. Put it over the frame. Tape the edges down inside the coracle.

You could make pipe cleaner people to go inside.

▲
Cut a strip of card. Tape it inside the coracle to make a seat. Float the finished coracle in a bowl of water.

3

Travel in Ancient Egypt

The Egyptians lived on the banks of the River Nile. The easiest way for them to travel was by boat along the river.

Trading boats

Wooden boats took grain, ropes and jewellery to Byblos and other towns near the Mediterranean Sea. They carried silver, oils and wood back up the Nile.

The wind blew against a huge sail and pushed the boat along. When the wind was blowing the wrong way, sailors took the sail down and rowed the boat.

Mediterranean Sea
Byblos

EGYPT

River Nile

North
W E
S

This map shows Egypt.

Sailors used a weighted rope to check how deep the water was.

Trading boat with its sail up.

Front

Trading boat with its sail up.

The back of the boat was carved to look like an Egyptian flower called a lotus.

Going north and south

The wind usually blew southwards along the Nile. Ships going south could use their sails while ships going north were rowed with their sails down.

Going north

Going south

Egyptians were so used to this that in their picture writing a ship with its sail up meant going south. A ship with its sail down meant going north.

This man is using a paddle to move the boat along.

Hunting boat

Hunting boats

Smaller boats were used for hunting water birds and fishing. They were made out of bundles of reeds tied together.

Cats were trained to help people hunt birds.

Reeds hold a lot of air so they floated very well.

Sailors pushed these paddles into the water to steer the boat.

Trading boat being rowed.

This thick rope helped to make the boat strong.

Front

Oarsmen faced the back of the boat.

Each oarsman pulled an oar to make the boat go forward.

A travelling god

The Egyptians believed that the sun was a god called Ra. They thought he travelled in a magic boat that flew across the sky.

Sun god

Travel on land

The Nile flooded every year so its banks were often muddy. The rest of the land was sandy desert. It was difficult to travel over the mud and sand. Here are some of the ways Egyptians did it.

Donkeys

Traders loaded donkeys with baskets so they could take goods across the ▶ desert to swap or sell.

Travelling chairs

◀ Rich people got servants to carry them in travelling chairs called palanquins.

Palanquin

Sand sledges

People pulled heavy loads on sledges. Sometimes they put rollers underneath to help the sledge slide more easily. ▶

Rollers were moved to the front.

Faster travel

Chariot

3,700 years ago, the Hyksos people* invaded Egypt. They used chariots pulled by horses. The Egyptians were amazed by the speed of these chariots. Rich Egyptians began to use them for hunting and fighting.

*These were a tribe that came from Asia.

Going on a Roman road

The Romans came from Italy and conquered many lands in Europe and North Africa. They built over 80,000 kilometres of roads across them.

All sorts of people travelled across the lands. Everyone could go more easily on smooth Roman roads than over rough ground or paths.

Soldiers could march 30 kilometres in one day.

Soldiers marched to every land to keep order there.

Chariot races

In Rome and other cities, chariot races were held on race-tracks. Many people watched them. They used to bet on which driver would win.

Messengers rode non-stop on horses or in fast chariots.

Poor people walked. They could not afford to travel any other way.

Chariot

How the Romans built a road

Builders worked out the shortest route. They built the road along it like this:

1. They marked the way by lighting fires which could be seen from a distance.

2. A trench was dug between the fires. It was at least six metres wide.

3. They packed the trench with layers of broken stones, gravel and sand.

4. They covered the top with large, flat stones called paving stones.

Crossing rivers

Some roads went through shallow rivers. People had to wade into the water. These crossing places were called fords.

Ford

Roman bridges are called viaducts.

Romans built bridges over deep rivers. They made them by building strong arches out of brick or stone.

Arch

Romans measured long distances in marching steps. On roads, a stone marked every 2,000 steps so travellers could see how far they had gone.

Stone

Crossing the sea

Galley

Trading ship

Galleys had oars and sails to make them go quickly.

Many Roman lands were on the edge of the Mediterranean Sea. Trading ships carried wine, wood and other goods between them.

Pirates sometimes attacked these ships. The Roman navy used fast ships called galleys to catch and fight pirates.

Groups of people could ride inside covered carts.

People sometimes pulled carts.

Inn

Camels carried goods across sandy deserts where people could not build roads.

Thanking the gods

Travelling was dangerous as bandits hid along some roads. If a traveller had a safe journey he thought the gods had helped him. Many travellers thanked their gods by putting up statues of them.

Traders used oxen to pull heavy loads.

Some rich people got slaves to carry them in a litter.

Litter

Slaves

There were inns along the roads so travellers could rest. Messengers changed horses at inns so they could keep riding quickly.

Many people camped in tents instead of going to inns.

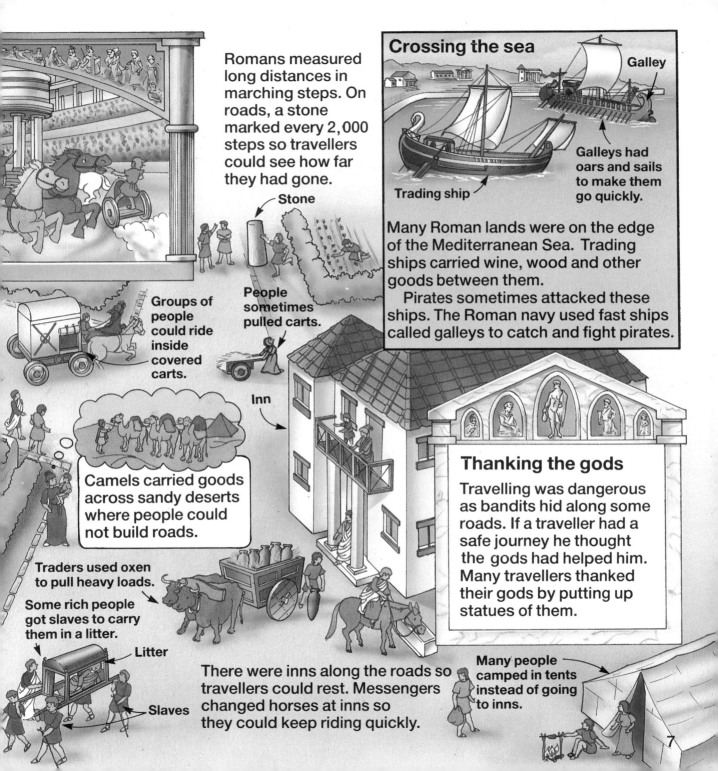

Chinese ways

China is a huge country. People worked out all sorts of ways to travel across it.

Maps

Chinese maps were made from layers of wood. The layers were built up thickly in places to show where the hills were.

Hills

Painted river

They built bridges over steep valleys. They made them by hanging a wooden walkway from ropes. This type of bridge is called a suspension bridge. ▼

Ropes

◄ Builders made firm stone roads so horses and carts did not get stuck in mud or fall over bumps.

People fixed umbrellas on carts to give shelter from the rain and sun.

Stirrups and padded saddles made riding more comfortable.

Statue

Soldiers

Stirrup

Travellers taking tea by the roadside

Machinery

Soldiers marched to all parts of China to keep everyone in order.

Some took along a carriage with a statue on top. The statue always pointed south. This helped the soldiers find their way.

The statue looked as if it worked by magic. In fact, machinery hidden inside the carriage turned the statue when necessary.

Moving home

Some people lived in felt tents on plains at the edges of China. They herded animals and had to move around to find grass for them. People like this who move around a lot are called nomads.

Tent packed on camel.

The Great Wall of China

The Chinese built a huge wall to keep enemies out of China. It was so big, people could travel on top of it.

Travelling by junk

Boats called junks carried people and goods along rivers. Some junks sailed across the sea to other countries such as India.

Junks like this one are still used in China today.

People put sails on wheelbarrows so the wind helped move heavy loads.

Some balanced awkward loads on poles so they could carry them easily.

Dangerous rivers

Some rivers were rocky and flowed so quickly that it was dangerous for junks to sail on them. Instead, people put on harnesses and pulled the junks along.

Sails had wooden strips inside to make them stiff.

The rudder was turned to the left or the right to steer the ship.

People slept and ate under these covers.

Viking sailors

The Vikings were brave sailors. They sailed along rivers and across seas to many European countries and to America.

This map shows the ▶ countries Viking sailors reached from their homelands in Sweden, Denmark and Norway.

Norway
Greenland
Sweden
Russia
America
British Isles
Denmark
France
Spain
Italy
Istanbul
Mediterranean Sea
N
W E
S

A flag showed the sailors which way the wind was blowing.

Vikings often made trips to buy and sell goods. But sometimes they set out to attack and rob. Then they used boats with carved dragon heads. They hoped these would scare enemies.

Carved dragon head

Viking robbers captured animals as well as treasure.

Vikings used boats like this to make their surprise attacks.

Sailors kept their belongings in chests.

At night sailors slept in skin sleeping bags.

The boat wasn't very deep. This was so it could sneak up shallow rivers.

Vikings made their boats from wooden planks. They were nailed on top of each other so they overlapped.

Nails

Sheep's wool and tar were stuffed between planks to keep water out.

Sailors watched for certain birds and seaweeds. If they saw them they knew they were near land.

10

Raven guides

A Viking called Floki Vilggerdarson used ravens to help him find land. He carried them on his ship and let them go one at a time.

If a raven flew off, Floki followed it. He knew it would fly to the nearest land. But if it returned quickly, he knew there was no land near.

The boat was steered with a broad paddle called a steerboard.

Travel on land

The Vikings were used to travelling in cold northern countries. They used skates, skis and sledges for crossing ice and snow.

Many sledges were pulled by horses. Vikings fitted spikes to the horses' hooves. This gave them a good grip on the ice.

Spike

Oars

◄ Vikings used oars to row boats along when there was no wind or they wanted to make a fast get-away.

Cover

Oars went through holes in the side.

Sailors pulled ropes to turn the sail so it caught the wind.

Sailors from Arabia

While Vikings were sailing around Europe, Arabs were sailing to East Africa, India and China. Arab sailors told strange stories about the places they found. These were written down in a book you can still read, called 'The Voyages of Sinbad the Sailor'.

These triangular sails caught more wind than the sail on a Viking boat.

An Arab ship

Travel in medieval Europe

People in Europe knew little about the rest of the world. Some travellers went a little way into Asia and Africa but most kept to the lands near the Mediterranean Sea.

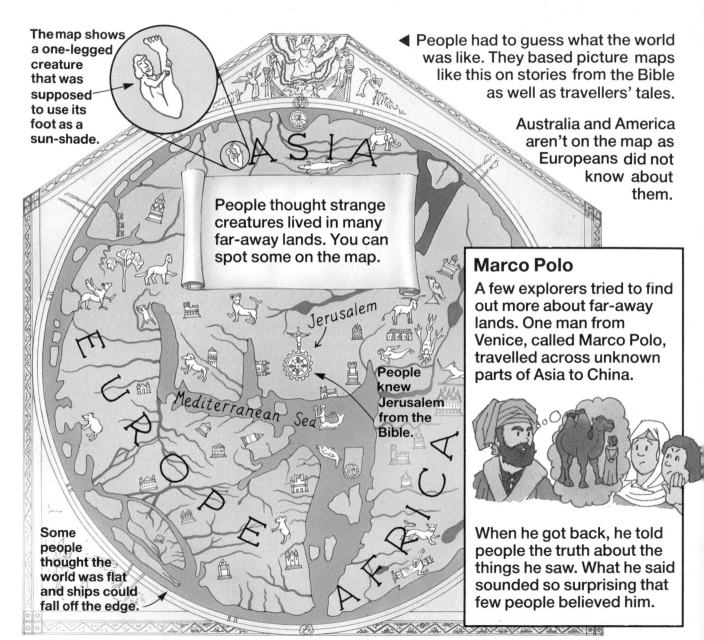

The map shows a one-legged creature that was supposed to use its foot as a sun-shade.

◀ People had to guess what the world was like. They based picture maps like this on stories from the Bible as well as travellers' tales.

Australia and America aren't on the map as Europeans did not know about them.

ASIA

People thought strange creatures lived in many far-away lands. You can spot some on the map.

EUROPE

Jerusalem

Mediterranean Sea

People knew Jerusalem from the Bible.

AFRICA

Some people thought the world was flat and ships could fall off the edge.

Marco Polo

A few explorers tried to find out more about far-away lands. One man from Venice, called Marco Polo, travelled across unknown parts of Asia to China.

When he got back, he told people the truth about the things he saw. What he said sounded so surprising that few people believed him.

Buying bones

Pilgrims (see right) could buy dead saints' bones at many of the places they visited. They thought these bones had holy powers to help them. Some people tricked pilgrims by selling animal bones instead.

Many saints' bones were kept in boxes shaped like statues.

Pedlars, pilgrims, knights and other travellers

Even in European countries, travel was slow and difficult. But many people still made journeys for all sorts of reasons.

Roads and paths were full of holes and bumps.

Pedlars

People called pedlars travelled around towns and villages carrying goods to sell.

Pilgrims

People called pilgrims went to pray in places where saints had lived.

Rich people's coach

Knights

Knights and soldiers travelled to fight wars in different countries. There were many wars in the lands near Jerusalem.

Sailing ships took travellers across the sea.

Horses used for carrying things were called pack horses.

Some rich people were carried in a huge travelling box called a litter.

Ladies rode sideways as they wore long skirts.

Rich people

Rich families often had two or more homes. They travelled between them with their servants and friends.

Exploring by sea

Arabs and Turks fetched jewels, silks and spices by camel from Eastern countries such as India. They sold them for lots of money to people in Europe. Europeans began to find ways to the East by sea, so they could get these valuable things for themselves.

The first explorers were often frightened. They had to cross unknown seas in small ships. Nobody knew how far they had to go or if they would return.

Sailors stood here to keep watch for land.

Ships were only about 30 metres long. That's about the length of three buses.

An explorer's ship being loaded for a journey.

There was only room for a few animals. They were soon killed and eaten.

Proving the world was round

Many people still thought the world was flat (see page 12). Long sea journeys began to show that the world was round like an orange. This was finally proved when Magellan's ship sailed all the way round the world in 1519-1522.

Some explorers' voyages are marked on this globe. ▶

Magellan died on the way but his ship carried on.

Columbus meant to sail round the world to India in 1492. He landed in the West Indies by mistake.

Vasco da Gama sailed around Africa in 1497.

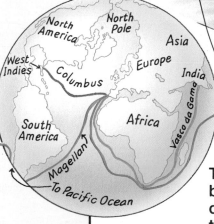

North America
North Pole
Asia
Europe
West Indies
Columbus
India
South America
Africa
Vasco da Gama
Magellan
To Pacific Ocean

They took lots of salted pork, biscuits and water to eat and drink. Some took animals so they could have fresh meat at first.

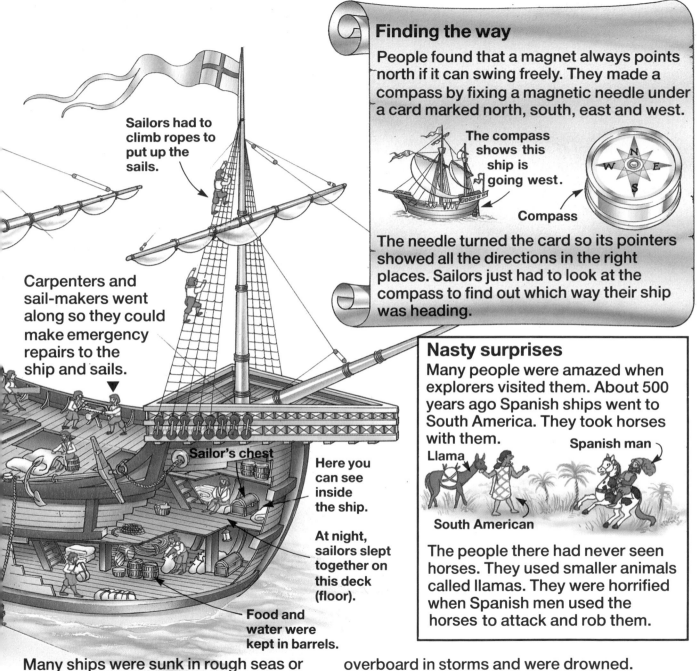

Sailors had to climb ropes to put up the sails.

Carpenters and sail-makers went along so they could make emergency repairs to the ship and sails. ▼

Sailor's chest

Here you can see inside the ship.

At night, sailors slept together on this deck (floor).

Food and water were kept in barrels.

Finding the way

People found that a magnet always points north if it can swing freely. They made a compass by fixing a magnetic needle under a card marked north, south, east and west.

The compass shows this ship is going west.

Compass

The needle turned the card so its pointers showed all the directions in the right places. Sailors just had to look at the compass to find out which way their ship was heading.

Nasty surprises

Many people were amazed when explorers visited them. About 500 years ago Spanish ships went to South America. They took horses with them.

Llama

Spanish man

South American

The people there had never seen horses. They used smaller animals called llamas. They were horrified when Spanish men used the horses to attack and rob them.

Many ships were sunk in rough seas or wrecked on rocks. Even if a ship got back safely lots of the sailors did not. Some fell overboard in storms and were drowned. Many died of scurvy, an illness caused by not eating fresh food for a long time.

300 – 200 years ago
Horse-drawn coaches

At first, coaches were heavy and awkward (see page 13). About 300 years ago, coach builders began to make coaches lighter and easier for horses to pull. People made long journeys in them. These often took several days or weeks.

▲ Only very rich people could afford their own coach. They paid lots of money for elegant coaches. They had servants to drive them.

Luggage was strapped on the top.

Here you can see inside the stage-coach.

A guard rode with the driver to help fight off highwaymen (see opposite).

A horn warned that the coach was on the way.

It was cheaper to sit in a basket on the back.

Driver

Passengers climbed these steps to get into the coach.

Stage-coach

Crowded beds

At night, stage-coaches stopped at an inn where passengers could sleep. In some inns, people had to share a bed with one or even two strangers. They had to share with bedbugs and fleas as well.

More people could afford to buy tickets for seats in stage-coaches like the one above. These made regular long journeys.

Stage-coaches got their name because they always made a journey in stages. They stopped every few hours, at inns, to change tired horses for fresh ones.

Horse-drawn boats

Heavy loads such as coal were put on flat boats called barges. These were pulled along rivers by horses on the banks.

Horses could pull heavier loads in barges than they could in carts. People built canals (man-made rivers) so barges could carry goods to places not on rivers.

Difficult and dangerous roads

In many countries, roads were rough and difficult to travel on. Few coaches could go faster than 12 kilometres an hour.

Some roads had huge stones, and puddles deep enough to drown in. Many coaches fell over on the rough ground, injuring and sometimes killing the passengers.

The driver flicked the horses with a whip to make them go faster.

The driver steered and stopped the horses by pulling on their reins.

Passengers were often uncomfortable. They sat squashed together. The coach swayed a lot so they bumped against each other.

The horses' tails were cut short to stop them getting tangled in the harness.

← Harness

A stage-coach was pulled along by four horses. The driver sat behind them. He had to be very skilful to control them all.

Highwaymen

Highwaymen were robbers on horseback. They attacked coaches. They threatened to kill passengers unless they gave up their money and jewels.

Travelling across North America

Before this time, many Europeans had come to live in North America. Most stayed near the East coast where their ships had landed. Then explorers found ways to the West. Families now began to cross America in search of land to farm and live on.

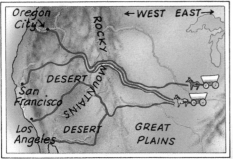

Travellers had to go over mountains, wild plains and deserts. This map shows some of the ways they went.

People travelled in covered wagons pulled by oxen. They took tools and furniture to help them set up their farm homes.

They had to take lots of food and water for the long journey.

A plough for the family's new farm

Water barrel

Farm animals followed behind the wagons.

Wheels often broke on the rough ground. Travellers had to know how to mend them.

Cowboys

Some settlers became cowboys. These were men who rode horses to herd cattle on the plains. They rode hundreds of kilo-metres each year.

Dangers and difficulties

Sometimes Indians attacked wagons. People travelled in groups so it was easier to fight them off.

Fierce dust storms blew up on the plains. The winds were so strong they overturned some wagons.

Travellers got wagons across rivers by taking their wheels off and letting them float over.

The Pony Express

In 1860, a quick mail service started between the West and the East. This was called the Pony Express. Riders carried the mail on fast ponies. Fresh ponies were kept at stages so riders could change on to them and keep going at full gallop.

People often had to get out and walk. This made it easier for the wagon to go over rocky ground.

Oxen were strong but slow.

The journey took several months. During that time the wagon was a family's only home. They ate and slept inside it.

Travelling Indians

Indians had lived in tents on the plains for many years. They moved around to find buffalo to kill for food.

They took their tents with them when they moved. They folded them and put them on frames. Ponies dragged the frames along.

Taking the train

In 1869, a railroad was built across America. It was 5,319 kilometres long. Then people could travel West in comfortable trains.

19

Using steam power

During this time, inventors began to make new machines for people to travel in.

They used steam to power many of these machines.

Early steam trains

Early steam trains seemed very fast to people used to horse-drawn vehicles. Many people were frightened that the speed would kill their passengers. ▼

Smoke from the fire came out here.

Driver

Stoker

Trains needed to carry lots of coal or wood for the engine.

Stephenson's 'Rocket'

The wheels ran along iron rails so the train travelled smoothly.

George Stephenson's 'Rocket' was a famous early train. People were amazed at its speed of 48 kilometres an hour.

How a steam engine works

A fire heats water in a tank. When the water ▶ boils it turns to steam. The steam rushes along a pipe and pushes a rod called a piston. This is joined to the wheels. The piston turns the wheels as it moves.

Travelling by steam train

A train's carriages were pulled by a steam engine. A man called a stoker shovelled coal or wood to keep a fire going inside it.

This first class carriage has glass windows.

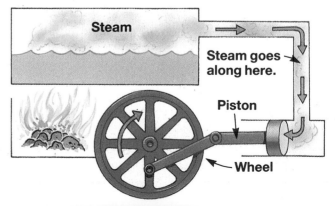

Steam

Steam goes along here.

Piston

Wheel

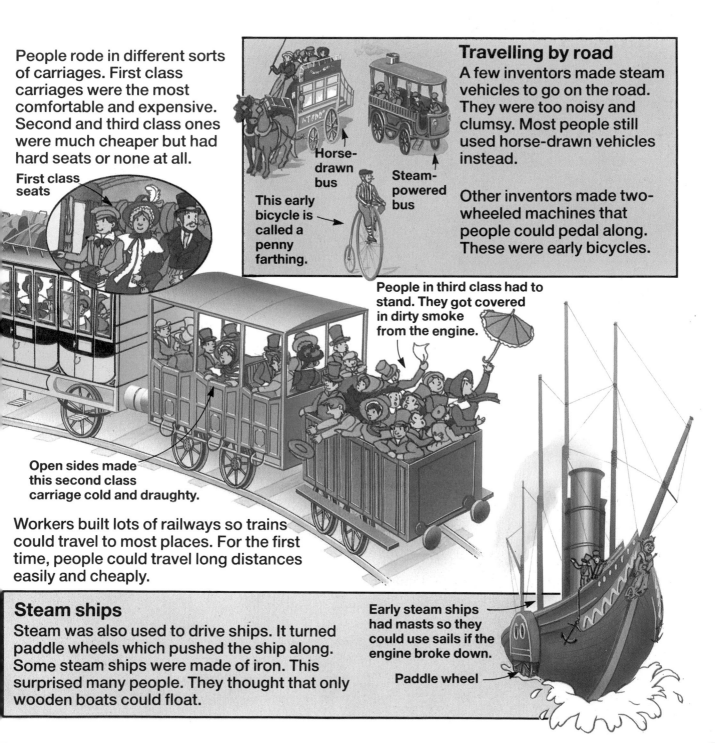

People rode in different sorts of carriages. First class carriages were the most comfortable and expensive. Second and third class ones were much cheaper but had hard seats or none at all.

First class seats

Travelling by road

A few inventors made steam vehicles to go on the road. They were too noisy and clumsy. Most people still used horse-drawn vehicles instead.

Other inventors made two-wheeled machines that people could pedal along. These were early bicycles.

Horse-drawn bus

Steam-powered bus

This early bicycle is called a penny farthing.

People in third class had to stand. They got covered in dirty smoke from the engine.

Open sides made this second class carriage cold and draughty.

Workers built lots of railways so trains could travel to most places. For the first time, people could travel long distances easily and cheaply.

Steam ships

Steam was also used to drive ships. It turned paddle wheels which pushed the ship along. Some steam ships were made of iron. This surprised many people. They thought that only wooden boats could float.

Early steam ships had masts so they could use sails if the engine broke down.

Paddle wheel

Going further and faster

New inventions quickly replaced old ways of travel. Cars were used instead of horses to go over land. Faster ships were used on the sea. Planes and airships flew through the air. People could travel more easily than ever before.

Travelling by car

The very first cars were expensive. Then, in 1909 Henry Ford began to make cheaper cars in efficient factories.

Many people could now afford to buy their own car. Travel became so easy that people often made journeys just for fun.

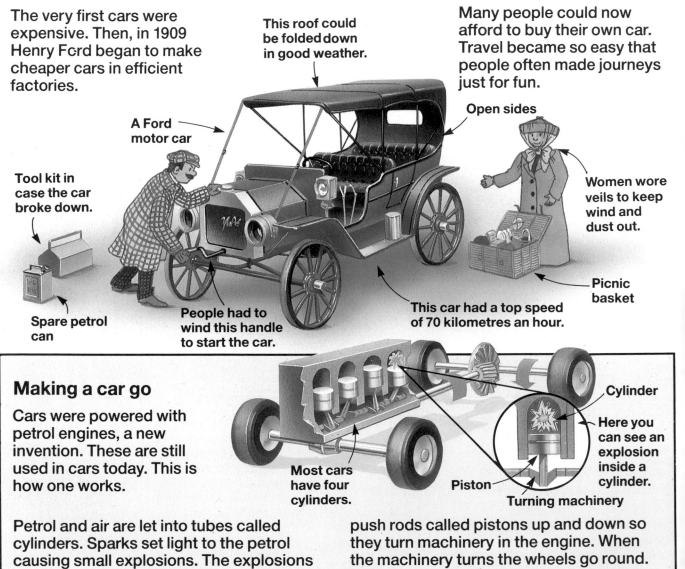

This roof could be folded down in good weather.

A Ford motor car

Open sides

Tool kit in case the car broke down.

Women wore veils to keep wind and dust out.

Spare petrol can

People had to wind this handle to start the car.

This car had a top speed of 70 kilometres an hour.

Picnic basket

Making a car go

Cars were powered with petrol engines, a new invention. These are still used in cars today. This is how one works.

Most cars have four cylinders.

Cylinder

Here you can see an explosion inside a cylinder.

Piston

Turning machinery

Petrol and air are let into tubes called cylinders. Sparks set light to the petrol causing small explosions. The explosions push rods called pistons up and down so they turn machinery in the engine. When the machinery turns the wheels go round.

Flying through the air

Some people had invented flying machines before this time. Most could only hop off the ground. Others like balloons could not be steered very well. ▶

Early glider

Balloon

Airships were the first machines to fly travellers wherever they wanted to go. People sat in cabins below a long gas bag. Propellers pushed the airship along. ▶

Airship

Passenger cabin

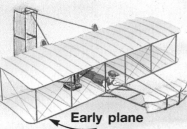

Early plane

Plane in 1936

Helicopter in 1938

The first real aeroplane was called 'The Flyer'. It was made and flown by Wilbur and Orville Wright in 1903. Later inventors improved on their work.

By 1936, planes could carry passengers at about 300 kilometres an hour. Today, jet planes carry people at 1,000 kilometres an hour to places all over the world.

Another invention, the helicopter, could land in less space than a plane. It is still used to fly people to places in mountains or jungles where planes cannot land.

Moon buggy

Landing craft

Flying to the moon

About 30 years ago, inventors made rockets to take people into space. In 1969, Buzz Aldrin and Neil Armstrong were the first to reach the moon. Since then ten more people have made this 384,000 kilometre journey.

Sea travel

People began to use submarines like this to explore under the sea. The deepest anyone has been so far is about 11 kilometres down. ▼

Huge passenger ▲ ships called liners were built. These are still used today. They can carry several hundred people at a time.

Index

First published in 1990
by Usborne Publishing Ltd,
Usborne House,
83-85 Saffron Hill,
London,
EC1N 8RT,
England.

Printed in Belgium.